Tom Coulter
19 Sunwich St.
Belfast

THE
INCREDIBLE
BOOK
EATING
BOY

Liverpool

✓ Chester   16

a 540   a 529
Wrexham 12
a 828   Whitchurch 20
Shrewsbury 28   a 529

                 a 442

a 458   Wellington   22
                 a 442

⑦ Bridgnorth 20 Bridgnorth   14   ⑦
                 a 442

                 Kidderminster 13
                 a 422

                 Worcester   ·14
                 a 38

                 Tewkesbury   15
                 a 38

                 Gloucester   11
                              ───
                              125

For Tommy and Kathleen

FIRST PUBLISHED in HARDBACK
in Great BRITAIN by HARPERCOLLINS
children's BOOKS in 2006.

13   5   7 9   10   8   6 4 2

ISBN - 13:978-0-00-718 227 - 5
ISBN - 10: 0-00-718227-9

HarperCollins Children's Books is a division of HarperCollins Publishers Ltd.
Text and illustrations copyright © Oliver JEFFERS 2006
The author/illustrator asserts the moral right to be identified as the
author/illustrator of the work. A CIP catalogue record for this
title is available from the BRITISH LIBRARY.
Fulham Palace Road, Hammersmith, LONDON W6 8JB
www.harpercollinschildrensbooks.co.uk

printed and bound in CHINA.

THE
INCREDIBLE
BOOK
eating
BOY

by Oliver Jeffers

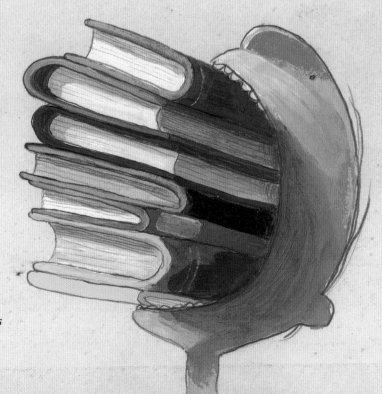

 HarperCollins *Children's Books*

HENRY

loved BOOKS.

But not like you and I love books, no.

Not quite...

...Henry loved to *EAT* books.

It all began quite by mistake one afternoon when he wasn't paying attention.

He wasn't sure at first,
and tried eating a single word,
just to test.

Next, he tried
a whole sentence
and then the
whole page.

Yes, Henry definitely
liked them.
By Wednesday,
he had eaten
a WHOLE book.

And by the
end of the month
he could eat a whole
book in one go.

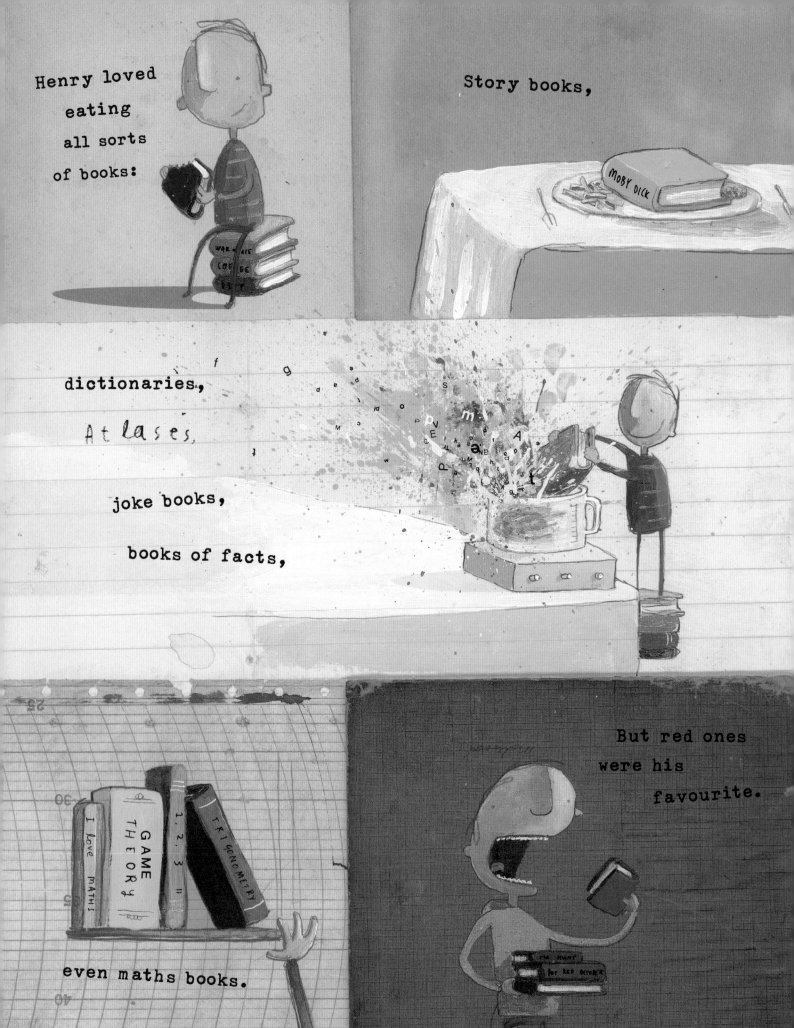

Henry loved eating all sorts of books:

Story books,

dictionaries,

Atlases,

joke books,

books of facts,

even maths books.

But red ones were his favourite.

And he was going through them at a fierce RATE.

But here is the best bit:

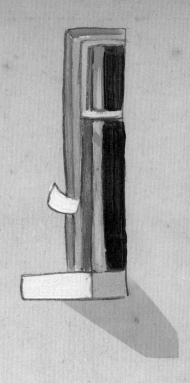

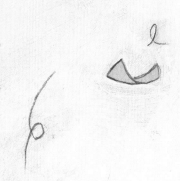

He ate a book
about goldfish
and then he knew
what to feed Ginger.

hmm?

MONUMENTAL

Before long he could do
his father's crossword
in the newspaper,

and was even smarter than his teacher in school.

Henry loved being smart.

He thought that if he kept going,

he might even become

the **smartest** person on Earth.

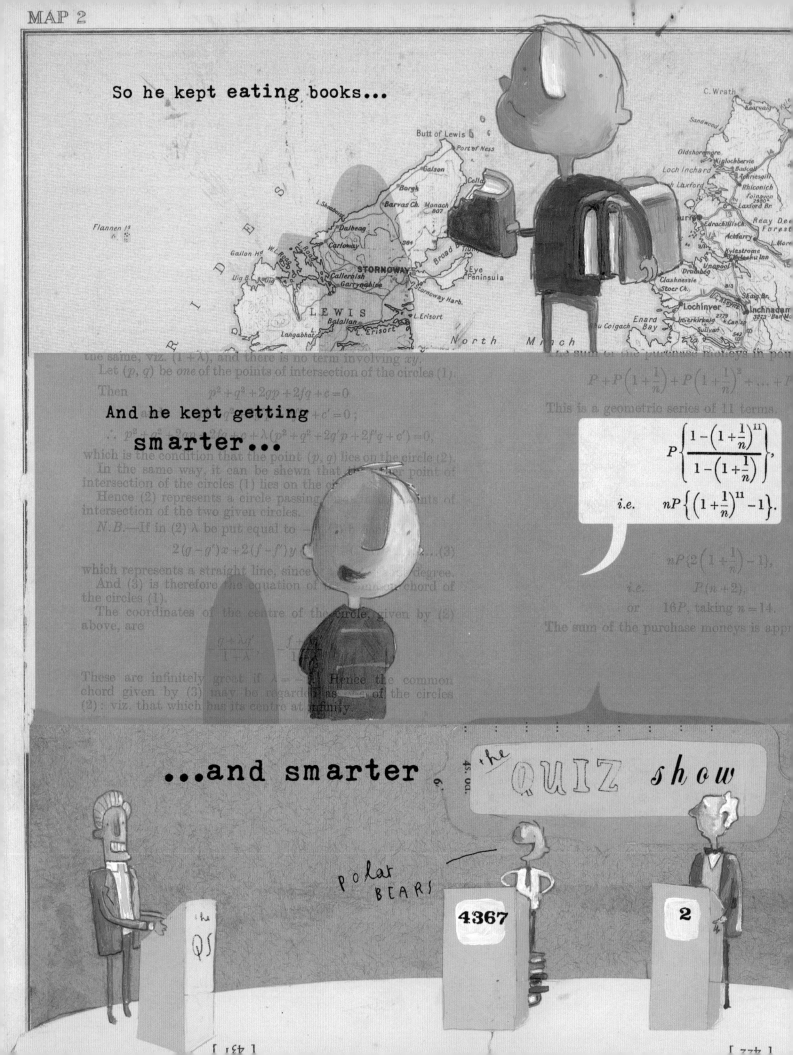

...and smarter.

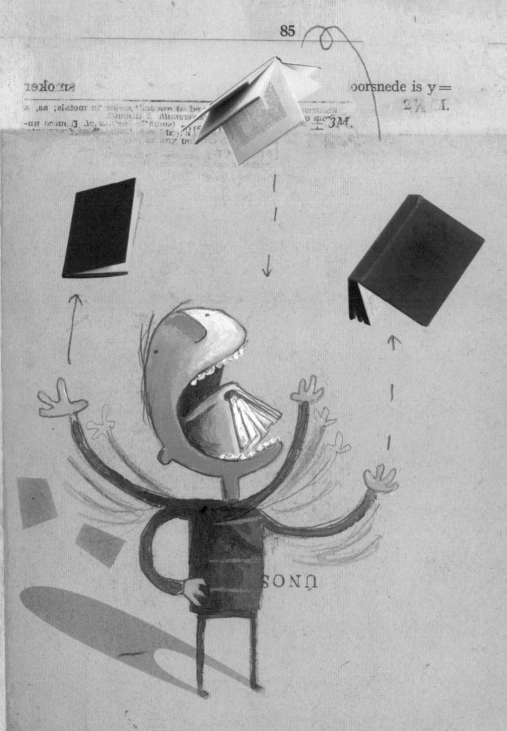

He went from eating books whole
to eating them three or four at a time.
Books about anything.
Henry wasn't fussy,
and he wanted to know it all.

But then things started going not quite so well.

In fact, they started going
very,
very,
wrong.
Henry was eating too many books,
and too quickly at that.

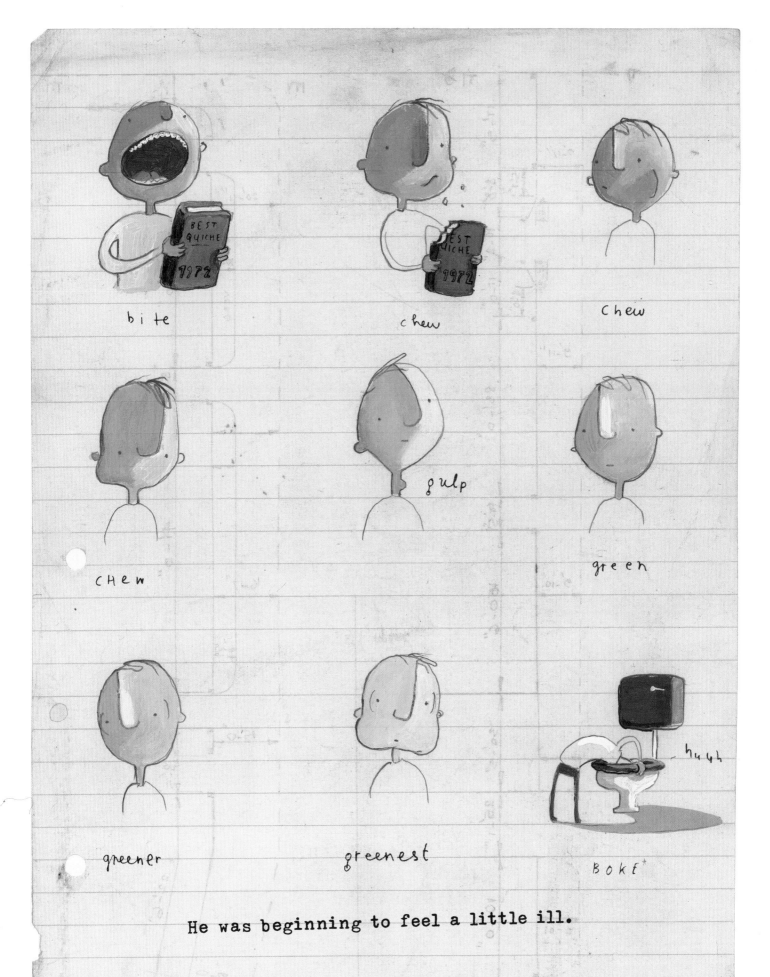

bite

chew

chew

chew

gulp

green

greener

greenest

huh

BOKE*

He was beginning to feel a little ill.

But here is the worst bit.

Everything he was learning

was getting mixed up...

6 + 2 = 3

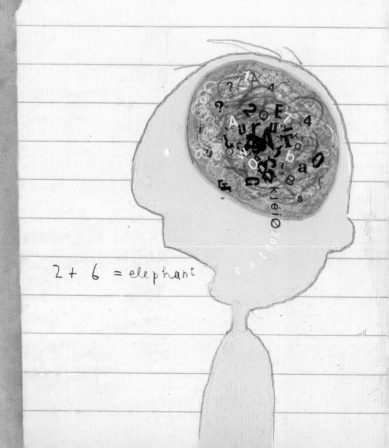

2 + 6 = elephant

he didn't have time

    to digest it properly.

It became quite embarrassing

    for him to speak.

20 exemplaires numérotés sur papier de Ho

Suddenly Henry didn't
feel very smart at all.

More than one
person told him
he should stop
eating books.

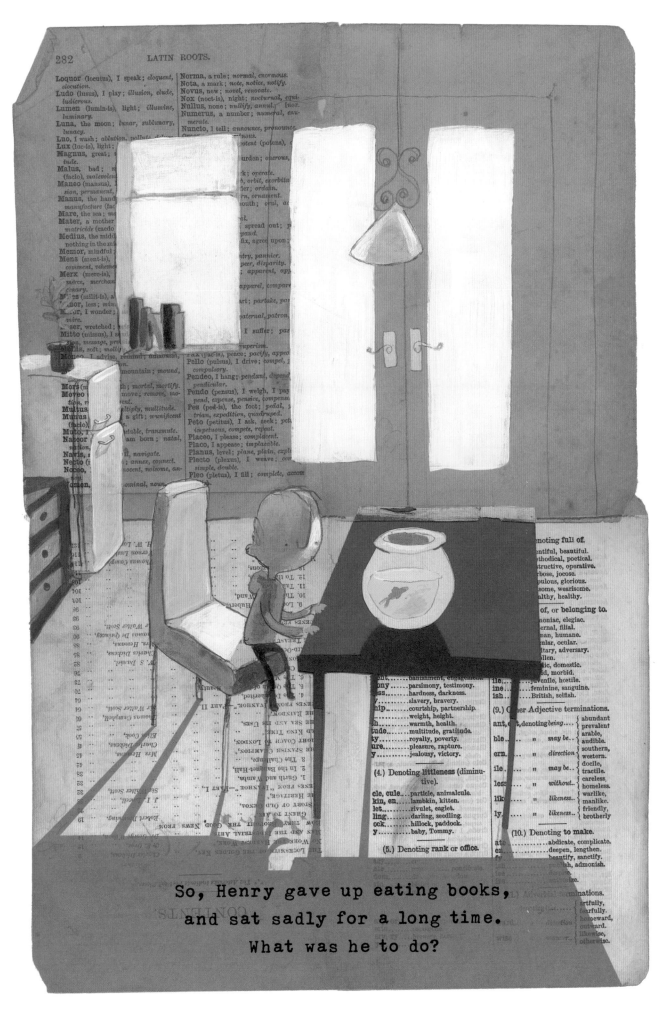

So, Henry gave up eating books,
and sat sadly for a long time.
What was he to do?

Then, after a while, and almost by accident,

Henry picked up a half-eaten book from the floor.

But instead of putting it in his mouth...

Henry
opened
it up...

...and began to read.

And it was **SO** good.

Henry discovered that he loved to read.

And he thought that if he read enough

he might still become

the smartest person on Earth.

It would just take a bit longer.

THE
INCREDIBLE
BROCCOLI
eating
BOY

Now Henry reads
all the time...

although every now and then